Albert is a little Pug who always gets himself into a pickle no matter what.

Not a single day goes by without someone saying to him "Oh Alby".

Albert has 3 brothers called Bruce, Robin and Tokie and 3 sisters called Biscuit, Chip and Lucky.

FastPrint
Publishing
http://www.fast-print.net/bookshop

OH ALBY
Copyright © Jodi Walker 2016

ISBN: 978-178456-406-3

First published 2016 by FASTPRINT PUBLISHING of Peterborough, England.

One morning Mummy Pug woke them all up with some exciting news. "Good morning puppies. As your birthday is one week away, each of you in turn will get to choose what activity to do on each day before your birthday. Now who should go first?" asked Mummy Pug. "Me, me, me!" all the puppies called, putting their paws up hoping to be chosen.

"Albert, as your name begins with the letter A, you can go first. What would you like to do today?" Mummy Pug asked.
"I want us to go fly kites in the park," Albert said.
So Mummy Pug took them to the park.

It was a very windy day and the perfect weather to fly kites. Suddenly the wind blew stronger and Albert was lifted off the ground.
"Mum, look at me I'm flying." Shouted Albert.
"Albert get down from there." Mummy Pug shouted back as her and the other puppies tried to grab Albert as he flew over their heads.

Suddenly, they all heard a big bang!
Albert had crashed into a tree and
tumbled to the ground.
All the puppies looked at him and
laughed.
"Oh Alby," they said.

On day 2, Mummy Pug said, "Biscuit, as your name comes next alphabetically, what would you like us to do today?"
"I would like us all to go for ice cream on the beach," Biscuit replied.
"Yes," all the other puppies cheered.
"I love ice cream," Chip smiled excitedly.

So that day Mummy Pug took them to the beach where they all sat in a row on the sand eating their ice creams.

Suddenly, the sand Albert was sitting on started to move and shake.
"It's an earthquake," yelped Albert,
throwing his ice cream into the air.
"I'm not an earthquake. You were sitting on my back!" said an angry
crab shaking Albert off.

All the other puppies looked at Albert and saw that the ice cream
had landed on his head and was dripping down his face.
"Oh Alby," they all said.

On day 3, Mummy Pug said, "Bruce, it is your turn. What would you like us to do today?"
"I want us all to go for a picnic by the river," Bruce replied.
So that afternoon they all sat by the riverside eating their picnic.

A frog jumped out of the water
and hopped into Albert's lunch
box and stole a sandwich.
Albert chased after him,
leaping from side to side until the frog
jumped back into the river and onto
a lily pad.
"You can't catch me now," said the frog
sticking his tongue out.

"Oh yes I can." Replied Albert as he jumped onto the lily pad.
Sadly, he was too big for the lily pad and it sank.
"Where did Albert go?"
Asked Mummy Pug.
"There he is." Laughed the puppies as Albert was stood in the river with the naughty frog sitting on his head.
"Oh Alby". Said Mummy Pug.

On day 4, Mummy Pug said, "Chip, it is your turn. What would you like us all to do today?"
"I want us all to go skateboarding," Chip replied, already holding her skateboard.

Mummy Pug took them to a nearby park and one by one they whooshed down the hill. As Albert skated, he became distracted by the smell of hot dogs coming from a stand nearby and decided to head towards it. But because he was going too fast, he couldn't stop.

"Look out!" Yelled Mummy Pug.
But it was too late. Albert crashed into the
stand sending hot dogs flying everywhere and
landing in front of his brothers and sisters.
"Is anyone hungry?"
Laughed Albert seeing the hot dogs lying
everywhere. All the puppies rolled on the
ground laughing as they said together,
"Oh Alby."

On day 5 Mummy Pug said,
"Lucky, today is your turn to pick
what we do. What will it be?"
"Today I want us all to go to the
fun fair." Replied Lucky.
So Mummy Pug and the puppies spent
the day at the fun fair.

All of a sudden a fly appeared and kept buzzing around Albert's head.
"Go away Mr Fly." Albert said waving his arms in the air.
But the fly wouldn't leave Albert alone and landed on his nose.

"ACHOO!!!." Albert sneezed. In doing so Albert's foot hit the pedal and it catapulted him out of the car and high up into the sky.

"Where did Albert go?" Mummy Pug asked.
"I'm over here." Called Albert sticking his head out from the bouncy castle he had landed on. "Oh Alby." Mummy Pug sighed.

On day 6 Mummy Pug said,
"Robin, it is your turn. What would you like to do?"
"I want us to go to the farm and feed the animals." Robin said.
So off they all went to spend the day at the farm.

"Look there are piglets." Albert said running to the piglet pen and pushing his head through a hole in the fence to get a closer look.
"Come on Albert we are going to feed the chickens." Called Robin.
Albert tried and tried but his head was stuck.

"I'm stuck." Albert cried
"Come on now Albert."
Said Mummy Pug.
"I'm stuck." Albert cried again.
"It's OK, I'll help you."
Said Daddy Pig as he waddled
over to see what all the fuss
was about.

"Ready, 1, 2, 3."
Said Daddy Pig as Albert
was pushed through the fence.
The force was so strong it
sent both Mummy Pug and
Albert soaring backwards and
they landed in a horse's trough.
"Oh Alby." Sighed Mummy
Pug shaking off the water.

On day 7 Mummy Pug said,
"Happy Birthday puppies you are 1 year old today. Now Tokie, it is your turn to decide what we do today."
"Today I want us to go and play football."
Said Tokie already wearing his football kit.

So off they all went to their local playing field.
It was boys versus girls and everyone was having a lovely time.
"Now Albert today is a special day and I don't want you having
any accidents." Said Mummy Pug as she pulled Albert to one side.
"I will be on my best behaviour."
Said Albert. And he was. For once Albert didn't get himself into a pickle.

However the day wasn't over yet and that evening when all the puppies' friends had arrived for the party they all sat around the dinner table to sing Happy Birthday. Mummy Pug brought out the cake which had seven candles on, one for each puppy to blow out.

"As Tokie went last with choosing
what you do this week,
we will go in reverse so he can
blow out his candle first."
Said Mummy Pug.
So one by one the puppies
took turns to blow out a
candle.

But then it was Albert's turn.
Albert stood on his chair so he could reach the cake when
suddenly the chair wobbled making him land face first
into the cake.

"Peanut butter flavour my favourite." Albert said licking his face. Mummy Pug, the puppies and all their friends looked at him and said together, "Oh Alby."

The End

Book 2 'The Littlest Pug' will be out in 2017. The story follows Albert's sister Chip as she learns great things can come from being small.

Follow Albert on Twitter: @Oh_Alby

Or email him: ohalbypug@gmail.com